Click and the Kids
Go Sailing

Charnan Simon

Illustrated by Richard Kolding

Cricket/McGraw-Hill

Amy   Martin   Click   Liz   the *Bumblebee*
                                            (the sitter)

Send all inquiries to:
McGraw-Hill Children's Publishing
8787 Orion Place
Columbus, OH 43240-4027

1-57768-885-6

1 2 3 4 5 6 7 8 9 10 RRD-W 05 04 03 02 01

Library of Congress Cataloging-in-Publication Data
Simon, Charnan.
    Click and the kids go sailing / Charnan Simon; illustrated by Richard Kolding.
        p. cm.
    Summary: Amy and Martin convince their babysitter Liz to take them sailing on her boat the *Bumblebee,* and Click the mouse goes along for the ride.
        ISBN 1-57768-885-6
    [1. Sailing—Fiction. 2. Brothers and sisters—Fiction. 3. Babysitters—Fiction. 4. Mice—-Fiction.] I. Kolding, Richard Max, ill. II. Title.
        PZ7.S6035 Cl 2001
        [E]—dc21
                                    00–011580

McGraw-Hill
Children's Publishing
A Division of The **McGraw·Hill** Companies

Martin and Amy had been waiting for summer for a long time.

"Well, Amy," said Martin. "Today is the first day of summer."

Amy nodded. "Yes, Martin, I know."

"You remember what that means," said Martin.

"Yes, Martin, I do."

Amy looked at Martin. Martin looked at Amy. "Liz!" hollered Martin.

"We need you!" shouted Amy.

Did someone say sailing? I'll be right back!

Liz came out on the porch. "What's up?"

"Last summer you said this summer we'd be big enough to sail in your boat," said Martin.

"We're big enough now," said Amy. "Would you take us sailing to Turtle Island?"

"Hmm," said Liz. "I did say that. And you *are* big enough now. But why Turtle Island?"

"The raspberries," said Amy, who liked to pick them.

"The raspberries," said Martin, who liked to eat them.

"Sounds good to me!" said Liz. "We'll sail to Turtle Island, pick berries, and then make raspberry ice cream."

"Let's go!" said Martin.

They were soon on their way to the lake.

"Can I help sail the boat, Liz?" called Amy. "I know all about sailing. I got a book from the library."

"I'll help, too," called Martin. "Or maybe I'll catch some fish. There are bass in that lake, you know."

"Martin!" said Amy. "You can't fish on a sailboat!"

There was a lot to do at the marina before they could sail. First, everyone put on life preservers.

"Orange, yuck," said Amy. "Aren't there any blue ones?"

Next, Liz found her equipment. "Here's my sail—and my rudder—and my daggerboard—and my paddle."

"What's a rudder?" asked Martin. "What's a daggerboard?"

"Things we need to steer the boat," replied Liz.

"Why do we need a paddle?" asked Amy. "I thought the wind was going to push us."

"Just in case of an emergency," said Liz.

"We won't need it," Amy assured Liz. "Real sailors don't use paddles."

"Pay attention, guys," Liz said. "This is how you get ready to sail." She put the daggerboard into its slot in the middle of the boat. She attached the rudder to the back of the boat. She raised the sail high.

"That's easy," said Amy. "I could do all that."

Martin looked at the *Bumblebee* bobbing on the water, ready to catch the wind and fly. "This is going to be great!"

"Now," said Liz. "Who wants to sit in back and help steer, and who wants to sit in front and tell us where to go?"

"I'll steer!" said Amy.

"That's OK with me," said Martin. "I'll sit in front and tell you how to get there." He pulled his fishing net from his back pocket. "Anyhow, it'll be easier to fish in front."

"Martin!" said Amy. "I told you—no fishing on a sailboat!"

First, Liz got Amy settled. "The back of the boat is called the stern. You can sit here and help me move the tiller. We push or pull on the tiller, the tiller turns the rudder, and the rudder turns the boat."

Next, Liz helped Martin. "The front of the boat is called the bow. It's the best seat in the boat—but you might get a little wet!"

Then Liz took her place. "OK, guys," she said. "A few rules. No standing up in the boat, no taking off your life preservers, and when I say 'Ready about!' get ready to duck. Then, when I say 'Hard alee!'—duck, fast! I'll be letting the sail sweep across the boat so we can turn. If you don't duck, you could get hit by the boom—that's this pole the sail is attached to—and that would *not* be fun!"

Hello, duck!

"Can I untie the ropes now, Liz?" asked Amy.

"Um, Amy," said Martin. "There aren't any ropes on a sailboat."

"Of course there are, Martin," said Amy. "Just look around!"

Liz shook her head. "Martin's right, Amy," she said. "Ropes are called lines on a sailboat. But how did you know that, Martin?"

Martin smiled. "I read Amy's library book."

Liz took one last look around. "I think we're ready," she announced. She unclipped the mooring line, turned the boat to catch the wind, and they were sailing!

The sun sparkled on the waves, and a breeze filled the sail. "Turtle Island, here we come!" announced Martin.

"I'm steering!" Amy called. "It's so easy! I can't believe I never knew how to do this before!"

"OK, " called Liz. "We're going to turn now. Ready about—prepare to duck!" She pulled the sail in close to the boat. "Now hard alee!"

The sail swept across the *Bumblebee,* just inches above Martin's head. "Hey!" he cried. "That was close!"

"Good ducking, Martin!" Liz said. "Now, Amy, let's push the tiller out—oops!"

"Yow!" Martin spluttered. "That was cold!"

"Sorry, Martin," Liz apologized. "But all real sailors get wet sometimes!"

"It's OK," Martin said. "It felt good!"

"What about me?" said Amy. "I'm a real sailor, too. I want to get wet!"

"Liz," Martin said, looking across the lake, "aren't we going the wrong way? Turtle Island is over there."

"Well," said Liz, "we can't sail straight into the wind, so we have to zigzag instead. It's called tacking. Amy, you and I will be very busy until we get to the island—and we'll all have a lot of ducking to do. Ready, guys?"

"Ready!" shouted Martin and Amy.

Tacking was fun. Every time Liz hollered "Ready about!" and "Hard alee!" Martin and Amy ducked, and the little boat turned. Left—right—left—right— the *Bumblebee* tacked its way across the lake until . . .

she stopped. The sail flapped half-heartedly, and waves lapped at the edge of the boat. Instead of skimming along, the *Bumblebee* rocked back and forth peacefully.

"How come we stopped?" asked Martin.

"We lost our wind," said Liz.

"It's still windy," Amy protested. "All the other boats are going."

"We didn't turn fast enough that last time," explained Liz. "Now we're pointed straight into the wind and can't go anywhere."

"We're going somewhere," said Martin. "We're going backward!"

It was true. Slowly and gently the *Bumblebee* was drifting backward in the wind. Martin reached over and dipped his net into the water. "Maybe now I can catch my fish," he said.

"Is this when the Coast Guard comes to rescue us?" Amy asked.

"Nope," said Liz. "We'll be fine. I just have to get us pointed the right way. Watch—first I let out this line—it's called a sheet—and push the tiller. Now the sail's filling up with wind again. Here we go!"

"Amy!" shouted Martin. "I almost caught a fish!"

It seemed like no time before the *Bumblebee* reached Turtle Island.

"Look, Martin," said Amy. "I sailed us all the way across the lake. Did you see how I did it? You can learn a lot if you watch me!"

But Martin was watching the shoreline. "Liz," he said, "there's no dock. How can we land?"

"Easy!" Liz said. "We're going to beach it!"

And Liz sailed the *Bumblebee* straight toward the beach until the bottom of the little boat crunched to a stop in the shallow water.

"Everybody out!" called Liz.

Amy and Martin jumped over the side of the boat and helped Liz pull it up onto the pebbly shore.

The raspberries on Turtle Island were even bigger and better and sweeter than Amy and Martin remembered. For a long time there was no sound but the rustling of bushes as they worked to fill their buckets.

Then Amy looked up. "Martin!" she scolded. "Your face is stained all red. Are you picking raspberries or eating them?"

"Both," said Martin. "Aren't you?"

Let's see—raspberry pie, raspberry tart, raspberry cobbler, raspberries with whipped cream . . .

It didn't take long to fill three raspberry buckets—even with lots of tasting. Almost before Amy and Martin knew it, they were getting back in the *Bumblebee* for the sail home.

"You watch the berries, Martin," said Amy. "I'll be busy sailing."

"OK, Amy," said Martin. He popped a handful of berries into his mouth. "I can do that."

"No tacking this time," said Liz. "We'll be running with the wind and going really fast. Hang on to your hats!"

Amy held on to her hat and helped Liz hold the tiller. Martin sat back to enjoy the ride and waved at everyone they passed.

They saw windsurfers and kayaks and canoes. "Hey, Liz," Martin said. "Canoe canoe? Get it? Can you canoe?"

They saw little sailboats like the *Bumblebee,* and one big, beautiful, white sailboat called the *Phantom Lady.* "Oh, my," said Amy. "That's the boat for me!"

23

The *Bumblebee* zipped back across the lake in the brisk wind. In no time Liz was pulling in close to the marina. "This will be trickier than beaching the boat on Turtle Island," she said. "We want to come right up to where we were before."

"I'll tie us up when we get to the dock," said Amy. She and Martin watched as Liz sailed the *Bumblebee* nearer and nearer to shore. It looked like a perfect docking, until . . .

a sudden gust of wind hit.

"My hat!" cried Amy. "The wind got my hat!"
She stood up—and reached—and bumped Liz—and
the *Bumblebee* sailed right past the end of the dock.

For a minute everyone was silent. They stared at the raspberries that had spilled all over the *Bumblebee* and into the water. "I'm sorry!" said Amy. "I wasn't supposed to stand up. What are we going to do?"

"Can we just take down the sail and pull the boat to the dock?" asked Martin. "The water's not very deep here."

"Good idea," said Liz.

"But our raspberries!" wailed Amy. "All our raspberries are spilled and we can't make ice cream!"

"There's an ice cream place by the marina," offered Martin. "Maybe we can stop for cones there."

"Another good idea," said Liz.

"Now I wish I'd eaten more berries while we were picking," said Amy.

Sorry to disturb you. We're just passing through. But have a raspberry!

"Too bad we didn't wear our swimming suits," said Amy. "Real sailors always get wet!"

"Hey," said Martin. "I almost got that frog!"

"No splashing!" said Liz.

"Sailing's fun!" said Martin. "Maybe next time I'll hold the tiller."

"I'll show you how," offered Amy. "Maybe next time I'll take out the *Phantom Lady*!"

"Maybe next time I'll bring lids for the raspberry buckets," said Liz. "But right now we need double-scoop waffle cones—with sprinkles. A first sail is something to celebrate!"

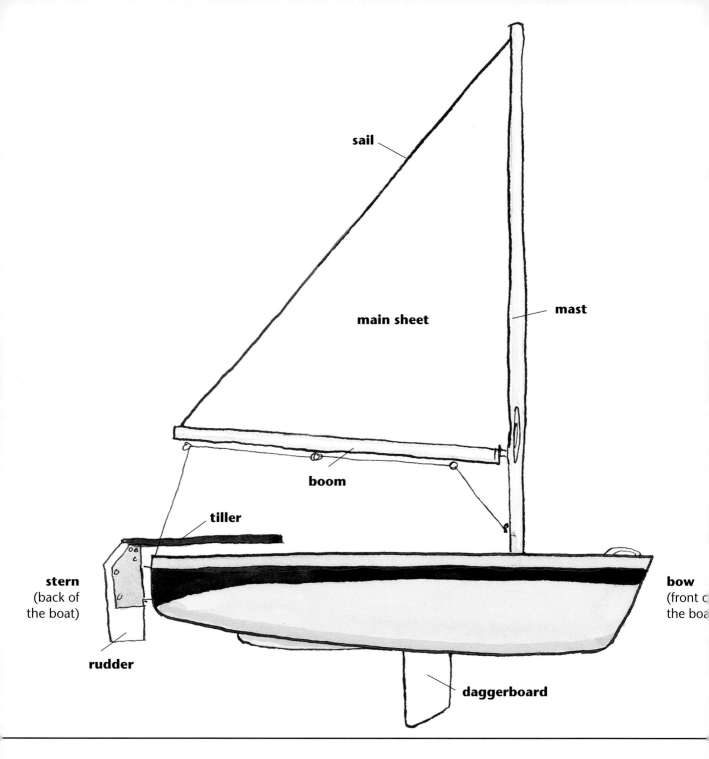

sail

main sheet

mast

boom

tiller

stern
(back of
the boat)

bow
(front of
the boat)

rudder

daggerboard

hard alee This is what the person who is steering says when he or she pushes the tiller toward the sail to turn the boat.

tacking This is what sailors do when they want to sail into the wind. Rather than sailing straight, they sail in a series of zig-zag beats.

ready about This is what the person who is steering says when he or she is getting ready to turn the boat. It warns the rest of the people on board that the boom is going to sweep across the boat.